Albatross

Love beyond infinity

AF380563

L S Ritika

ISBN 978-93-5458-978-2
© L S Ritika 2021
Published in India 2021 by Pencil

A brand of
One Point Six Technologies Pvt. Ltd.
123, Building J2, Shram Seva Premises,
Wadala Truck Terminal, Wadala (E)
Mumbai 400037, Maharashtra, INDIA
E connect@thepencilapp.com
W www.thepencilapp.com

All rights reserved worldwide

No part of this publication may be reproduced, stored in or introduced into a retrieval system, or transmitted, in any form, or by any means (electronic, mechanical, photocopying, recording or otherwise), without the prior written permission of the Publisher. Any person who commits an unauthorized act in relation to this publication can be liable to criminal prosecution and civil claims for damages.

DISCLAIMER: *This is a work of fiction. Names, characters, places, events and incidents are the products of the author's imagination. The opinions expressed in this book do not seek to reflect the views of the Publisher.*

Author biography

L S Ritika is a budding writer who aspires to become a hindi lyricist and a writer. She is a state level runnerup in creative writing. She is currently doing her undergraduation in science. Through her first novel "Albatross" she has tried to present a tale of moden love story that is raw to it's core. Her descriptive storytelling will take the readers through the roller-coster ride of a long distance relationship that has all the elements of humanly emotions.

CONTENTS

Epigraph

He loves her more than enough …

& she loves him beyond infinity…

Introduction

Life is beautiful. But it is not like that which we dreamt for. It is not like always the pleasant and peaceful one. Yes, it is beautiful but it is also true that it has its own dark side, the dark truth. Life itself is a hardest truth. But the painful moment of life become the blissful one with only the right person. It is such a blessing to have a person in life who can even listen your silence, sense your all emotions, hear all those things you never told even to yourself. The one who can feel you and the one to whom you can feel. With the right person, even your worst moments become magical and each moment of your life become special that you want to live those moments again and again and again. Each day become joyful and each moment become cheerful. Yes, it is true that there is a very bad and dark past in each person's life but it is also true that God sends his angels to lighten those dark past. And his angels set everything perfect, everything beautiful. With his angel every moment becomes special, each part of life is so precious and valuable so that one can live that moment peacefully and there will be no regret further in life for such moments.

Here I'm going to write a story, a beautiful one. May be mine, or maybe not. May be this one is real or maybe not. May be some parts are only fiction may be some parts are real one or maybe not ... But the emotions, the feelings are not false, not fake, those all are real, all are pure.

One

There is a very dark past present in everyone's life, which is as like as a painful trauma. It pierces heart each and every moment and make the wound alive until there is a person come into life to heal the wound. I had also such type of wound which engulf my heart even my soul completely. I had a broken and incomplete relationship which became a trauma for me. I got depressed for more than a year. I was unable to forget him. I punished myself, torture myself by not missing him, involving myself in all those thoughts which made me more depressed.

To overcome from this I started writing stories, songs, shayries. Whenever I felt pain I write shayries and through my words my pain got relief. I express my feelings by my words and also my pain got reduced. After some period of time I wished for a bright happy future and a beautiful one. Although I hated love but still there was a hope in any corner of my heart that one day would come when my pains got ended and I again would start my life from beginning.

I started narrated the parson of my dream in my poems. I wished that he would showered my life with pure love, true one. He might be like God's angel for me will come from heaven to brighten my life.

I started writing in an online writing app. I started sharing my shayries there. I was new to that platform. I posted my first shayri there and got very good response from different writers and after that there came more shayries from various other people. Then came a beautiful shayri from Prateek Bharadwaj. His writings were awesome. I stared following him. Then came some more shayries from more different different people. After sometime a shayri came from a person named Aman Kashyap. I read it. It was beautiful but some where it touched my heart. I could feel the emotion behind his writing. Then I started following him there. He posted his posts in certain intervals. I loved all of them. He became my favourite writer. It all were happened in the lockdown period of Corona pandemic situation.

Suddenly he stopped posting his writings in that app. I missed his beautiful notes. Then after some days he again started posting. I got overjoyed by seeing again his posts. So, I commented in his posts that where had he gone? His posts were awesome and I really missed them. He then replied me that thanks for complement and he now would going to post regularly. He then started following me. After seeing this why I didn't know but my happiness had no boundary. He then often liked my posts also. Whenever he liked my posts my mood become overjoyed.

He wrote a testimonial there before my birthday for the first time for me. After reading his shayri for me I felt like as if he knew me for many years, even though we did not know each other yet. His writing somehow confused me that how could be he wrote for me like this without knowing me as if he knew me for so many years.

Two

Till then I was like a phoenix who reborn from it's ash past but all I wanted to do was crash and burn. But somewhere at some point I was that albatross who searched his albatross eagerly.

After reading his testimonial I searched his profile in that app and visited through it. I saw his tiny pic there; it was not clear as well. He described his bio as devotee of Mahadev, from Bikaner, Rajasthan and a medical science student and health worker. The way he described his testimonial for me he attracted me. I loved his quotes. He gave his Instagram link there in his bio in that app. I started following him in Instagram from my Instagram page. In my Instagram page bio I gave the link of my personal account. I thought I should write him a testimonial to thank him for his beautiful testimonial for me. I wrote one for him. Then he liked that and also commented. We just did a small chit-chat there.

It was my Mom's birthday. The day was good but it was a very bad day for me cause I was betrayed by my friend. I was very much upset. I opened my personal Instagram account after a very long time. A follow request from Aman's Id appeared on my screen.

There was a big smile appeared on my face seeing this. I accepted it. I messaged him from my Instagram page "Hii."

"Do you remember me? It's me Ritu."

After few hours…

"Of course Yaar. How can't I recognize you! You are a beautiful soul. That's why I requested you on your personal Id to follow."

I was very happy by his answer, don't know why. We started chatting. It was not like a general chat. I texted him and he seen that and replied that after hours.

"Sorry dear I was very busy with my job. That's why I can't able to reply you and chat with you frequently. Really sorry for that." He texted me.

I replied "That's fine. No problem."

"Can we be friends?"

"We already are. Even best friends." He replied.

Three

I was very much happy to have his as a friend in my dull life. But also I had a fear to lose him. Although the relation between us was uncertain but still I felt something different which might be I never felt before.

"Hey, even we talked too much and are friends now but still I don't see you. Can I?" He asked me curiously.

"Why not." I replied. "I'm too not seen you yet."

"Okay, then you share your pic and also I." He said and I agreed.

I shared my pic first and after seeing this he replied "Ati sundar (Too much beautiful)."

He shared his. Although I never seen him before that but still I felt that I knew him very well.

I asked him, "Are you a model?"

"Nah!!" He replied.

"You look exact like any model Yaar. Too good."

"I liked photography and modelling as well but I'm not a model neither did it ever." He said.

He was too good, really. So handsome and too hot. Anybody could fall for him.

After reading his awesome quotes and being friendship with him his thoughts and behaviours attracted me most. And after seeing him might be I had something in my heart for him. Certain kind of unknown feeling.

I was completely alone at that period of time. Yes, I had many friends but I was surrounded by fake ones. My condition was somehow miserable. I wanted a person who would heal my broken soul and understood my pain, understood myself and become the reason of my smile. Some where I wanted Aman to become that one be.

I started feeling suffocated. I even unable to sleep at nights. Next morning I texted Aman "Will you be my Doraemon?"

Few hours later he replied, "I'll be happy to be that. If I'll be the reason of your happiness then it will be a great pleasure for me."

"Then I'll be the right over you and maybe I considered you as mine completely as a best friend. Are you agreed with this proposal? What say?" I asked.

"No problem. I'll be happy if you do all these. I'm all yours now and completely yours and only yours. Happy!!!" He replied.

I liked him very much and also never wanted to share him with anyone as well as I had a fear to lose him. I liked his company. I loved to talk with although we only talked through chatting.

"Do you never smile?" I asked.

"Why?"

"Cause I never seeing you smiling in any of your pics." I said.

He sent me some of his pics with little bit of smile. "What a smile man." I told to myself. I love my father's smile a lot in this whole world and that one is my favourite. But besides that Aman's smile was my favourite now. He looks too good. I felt like I lost myself somewhere in his smile. I loved that seriously.

We got more closer. I waited him to come online so that we could talk for a while. He had a very strict routine of time schedule of job from 9 am to 7 pm. Some days it exceeded the time also. That's why we faced very much difficulty to talk with each other ever for a while.

I thought he also liked me. The way he talked with me he expressed his somehow feelings were more than best friends.

"You know what Ritu, a boy and a girl can't be only friends for long term." Aman said me once.

"What do you mean? What do you want to say." I replied.

"Feelings will blossom both in our hearts very soon and it is real fact."

"It will never happened Aman."

"How can you be so sure?"

"I don't want to repeat the same mistake or maybe I don't bear the same pain again. I can control my feelings." I said.

May be at that point I could feel his love for me and also I could understood my feelings also and I had the fear that if the past repeats and if the situation arose and he would leave me. May be that's why I just didn't want a relationship. I didn't want to lose him either.

"Then it will be fine. And if feelings arise for me in your heart then please kindly inform me." Said Aman.

"Oh sure!!!"

Four

"Hey! Misthy what are you doing? Are you free. I wanna tell u sth." I texted Misthy.

Misthy was my bestie. Till then I didn't tell her anything about Aman. But I was confused now. I didn't want to get into a relationship and I didn't want to lose Aman as well. I also knew that Aman had also feelings for me in his heart. That's why I wanted some suggestion. Then I texted her.

It was a sunny day. Although it was August still it was a hot day. I texted Misthy at noon. She seen my message within fifteen minutes and replied me, "Yeah tell me! What happened?"

"There is a guy. I met him in an online app. He is a nice guy. Maybe I like him."

"Show me his pic."

I send her his pic. Then after sometime I deleted it from both device in whatsapp.

"How is he?" I asked.

"Wow yaar! Where did you get him. He is too handsome. Did he propose you? Say yes na. What do you think so much about it."

"He didn't propose me yet. But I think he likes me."

"Then what's that problem?"

"Do you please help me?" I asked.

"What? Say." She replied.

"I knew him hardly for a week. So, I don't know him properly neither we talked too much. Till now we are only friends. I want that can you please talk with him from your Instagram Id? I'll send you the link of his Id. Please talk with him and test him na whether he is a bad boy or a good one."

"Okay. I'll. Send me his Id." She replied. She texted him.

"Hey he is not replying Yaar." She said.

"He may be busy. He don't even talk with me today." I told her. "Please wait a while."

She talked with him later and send screenshots after.

"Ritu he is a good guy sweetheart. He is not a flirter at all. If he will propose you na then please say yes. Never let him go." Misthy replied.

Misthy told him that she was my bestie after sometime. I was very much happy to see all those chats. I was very happy because he was not a cheater or a liar. He was an honest person and I liked that too much. He was my crush now.

Five

During his conversation with Misthy he replied me first and also told me that another girl texted him whom he did not know. I too much astonished by his loyalty. He told me everything even then he did not know even Misthy was my friend. He impressed me with these small such things.

"Happy Janmastami mere Kanhaji." I wished him in Janmastami. It was a peaceful day. The weather was also calm and beautiful.

"Same to you Radhaji." He replied. "Btw, Radha and Krishna were lovers na?"

"Yeah, but Radha was Krishna's mami." I told him.

"Seriously."

"Yes. Didn't you know that." I said.

"No. Means you are my aunt now." He teased me.

"Shut up."

"Btw Ritu. You are the Shizuka and I am the Doraemon then who is the Nobita?" He asked.

"No one." I replied. "You are Nobita or Doraemon if I'm Sizuka?"

"I will like to be your Nobita." He said.

"That will be fine."

"But Nobita and Sizuka are boyfriend and girlfriend na and we are best friends right."

"Okay, leave it."

I believe strongly that he loved me by these statements.

Six

It was a nice sunny day. The weather was somehow pleasant. I travelled to my sister's house. It was a huge jungle by which the road passed through. Tall trees were standing both the sides of the road. Their shadows covered the road completely and hence the weather feels cool. Cool breeze blew and the music in the car made by mood jolly. I was travelling with my uncle but completely lost in the thought of Aman. I didn't know what kind of my mind and applied on me that he never leaved my mind and captured my thought whole day and whole night.

My aunt was very happy to see me and hugged me passionately. She kissed on my forehead and welcomed me home. My sister was also very much excited by my arrival. Their home was filled with laughter.

The dinner was over and it was too tasty. My aunt had magic in her hand that she made delicious foods. we talked for a while aunt, sister and me and then went to bed for sleep. I slept with my sister and aunt. At home I was unable to use phone at nights as it was strictly prohibited there. But there was no restrictions in my sister's house. And I had also a wonderful chance to talk with Aman at night peacefully as he was also free from his work at night.

I texted him, "Can we talk tonight? Are you free?"

He replied within ten minutes, "Of course dear. But how can you able to talk at night. Usually you don't come online at night na…"

"I'm not at my home today. I'm at my sister's home."

"When did you go?"

"Today." I replied.

We chatted very long time. Everything was okay and that night seemed to be beautiful for me.

"Do you like me?" He asked.

"Why?"

"Just for curiosity. Please tell na. We are best friends right and also very close to each other. Then you can tell me."

"Yeah, a little bit."

"Only little! Okay, that will be fine. I'm glad to hear at least that also." He said.

"Hey listen!" I replied, "Maybe I like you more than little."

"That's amazing Yaar. Thank you." He said with a great excitement.

"If you have any feelings for me more than just like, then you can also tell me that. I'm never gonna mind." He teased me.

"Do you like me?" I asked curiously.

"Of course yes. That's why I'm waiting for your text. Although I'm very busy all the day but still miss you and waiting for the moment when we talk." He replied passionately.

I started blushing by his reply. I was sure that he loved me. Now somehow I wanted to be more than friends but also I feared that there would be heartbreak in a relationship and also too much expectations which always hurts. But in friendship there is no such barriers.

"I think I'll make you my girlfriend. What say?" He teased me.

"What?" I exclaimed, "When did you fall in love with me?"

"Just kidding dear. Never mind. Btw there will be no problem if I make you my girlfriend. You are kind of sweet and beautiful and a nice girl. Then what's wrong with it." He replied.

"But there will be a problem if we get into a relationship. My schedule is too busy. So, I'll never give you that time which you deserve. That's why if we will get into a relationship then also it will not successful and you will be breaking up with me." He said.

"Aman!! I'm not that sort of girl who can't understand your situation. I know your schedule, your time management very well. I know that even you don't have time for yourself. I can understand you. But it will be best for both of us to be friends only, nothing else." I told him.

I told him that I wanted only friendship with him but at some point I also wanted that he convinced his feelings before me.

"Aman, daily I text you first. But tomorrow morning I want that you text me first." I told him.

"Okay dear! Done."

"Good ni8."

"Good ni8 dear. Take care." He replied.

My mind was full of excitement and my heart had like butterflies dancing. I was very very very much happy to know his genuine feelings for me. I wanted him in my life and also wanted to give our relation a name but still I had a but in my mind. My heart wanted him as a life-partner but my mind won't allow. There was a war between my mind and my heart the whole night.

Seven

I was excitedly waiting for the morning because Aman would going to text me. I was waiting for his message. My phone beeped and a message from his Id flashed on my phone screen.

"Good mrng dear." He texted.

"Very good mrng." I replied. "Whatsup?"

"I'm getting ready for work. Let's talk at ni8. May we?" He asked.

"Yeah sure! See you at ni8. I'll be waiting."

I eagerly waited for the night to come and the moment when we gonna talk. Each and every moment became special with him. I was started to live happy with his company. When he was with me I forgot all about my pains, my problems, the emptiness of my life. I just became happy during the time when he was with me. And the rest of time I was happy by recalling the beautiful moments we spent and by losing myself in his memory.

It was 10 o'clock sharp, the time for our conversation. I was waiting for him since 9.30 pm and it's been 10.15 pm today but still he did not come. It's 10.30 pm still he did not come online.

"What happened to him? Why did not he come online yet? Will everything be alright." I told myself.

His message flashed on my screen. "Hey! Sorry for being so late." He texted.

"It's ok. But why are you so late today? Is everything alright?" I asked curiously.

"Yeah everything is fine. But the thing is that I have a small fever. That's why I am so late today. I don't feel so comfortable na so …"

"What? How?? Did you check ur health to the doctor? Did you take medicine? Do u feel worse?" I asked him without even waiting for his reply.

"Don't worry dear. I'm fine. It's just a small fever. Why are you so worried about it?" He consoled me.

"Did u do ur duty today with having fever?" I asked.

"Yes." He replied.

"Why don't you take care of urself. U didn't not check doctor. Didn't take the leave from duty. How can u be so careless about ur health?" I said disappointedly.

"You are shouting like an angry wife." He said.

"I'm sorry. I didn't mean that."

"It's okay darling. It seems so good u care for me as my wife. Can I make u my wife?? What say?" He teased me.

"R u crazy? I cared u normally as a frnd. Nthng else."

"Nahh! It's not just like that. Not just like just frnd. You cared me as a wife. And I love that." He said. "Ritu, tell me what u want? Won't u love me?"

I was just surprized by his sudden question. I never expected that he asked me in this way.

"Do u love me?" I asked hesitantly.

"Of course." He replied.

"Of course what?"

"Of course, I love u Ritu. Please tell me what's ur feeling about this for me. Don't play with my emotions and feelings."

I became speechless. I wanted to said yes but I didn't know why I hesitated.

"I know u do. Then why are u quite. I want to hear it from you. Don't you love me Ritu answer me na."He said in a low tone and it sounds very sad.

"Yes. I do." I said finally.

"What? You do what? Ok leave it Ritu. I don't want to force u. You don't love me and that's ok. No need to say anything."

"Hey, it's not like that. I also love u ok. But the thing is that I don't wanna lose u." I exclaimed.

"I am never gonna leave u sweetheart. I love u sooo much and also I need u." He said.

Eight

"Do u want to be with me only as a girlfriend or want sth more?" He asked.

"What do u mean? I can't understand."

"I wanna be very close with u. I want u not as my gf. I want u as my wife. What say?"

"Okay. I agree. I'll be glad if u do that. But my parents will not agree for mrg."

"Aree. We will convince them na. And it is not matter who agree or not but for me u r my wife from now & forever." He said with a lot of confidence.

His confidence and grace won my heart every time. His elegance and behaviour everything not perfect but touched the core of my heart. He was very much special for me. After getting into a relationship with him I felt like the silent prayers of mine were fulfilled. I felt so lucky to have him in my life. He was just like an angel for me who showers me with all love and happiness. He changed my life completely.

"Aman you should take rest. You should sleep now." I said.

"No. Why? I'm ok don't worry."

"No. U have fever and u also did a lot of work today, a full day duty. U should take rest. We will talk tomorrow."

"No, I'm okay. I have taken medicine and I'll be fine by tomorrow. U just don't worry my wife." He replied so sweetly.

I was amazed by his words and also my heart filled with great happiness. That was the best night ever. Like all the happiness he showered on me. We talked late night.

Nine

"Ritu. Get ready as soon as possible. Your brother-in-law is on the way. They will arrive at any moment." Aunt said me.

My sister's in-laws were coming to take her back to her home. My sister came to her father's house on a casual holiday and now it's the time for her to go back her home.

I was getting ready before their arrival. "Hey kids, they are arrived. Go and welcome them." Uncle said to me and my cousin. I and Subha (brother) went to welcome the in-laws of my sister.

"Who's this pretty girl. She is too beautiful. She has dimples on her cheeks also. Who's this?" Sister's mother-in-law and father-in-law asked aunt curiously.

"This is my brother's daughter. They live in the town." Uncle introduced me to them.

"What is she doing and why she is wearing a turban on her head?" Asked her mother-in-law curiously.

"She is doing her graduation and she cut her hair very short. That's why she is wearing that turban." replied aunt.

I didn't know why but they took more interest in me.

"If I have a younger son then definitely I will make her my daughter-in-law." Said sister's mother-in-law.

I smiled but in my mind I thanked God for she had having only one son. She liked me very much and it made me upset. Usually when you started doing your graduation or reach the age of 20 plenty of marriage proposals start coming for you if you are a girl. It is a very bad culture in Indian villages specially.

We finished our meal and it was a delicious one. Everything was just perfect and tasty. I enjoyed the meal and so everyone.

"Let's go for a ride, me, you and your sister, what say?" My brother-in-law invited me.

"Yeah sure." I replied excitedly.

As before that I never met my brother-in-law before and never got a chance to talk with him or did some pranks, it was a great opportunity for me to do some fun.

"Okay, then go and take permission from father." He said to me.

"Who? Me? I'm going no where then. How can I get permission from uncle."

They both laughed. Brother-in-law asked aunt for permission and she agreed. We went for a ride in his Volkswagen.

The climate was just perfect and so romantic. It was cloudy and cold breeze blew and each time it touched my body it refreshed my mind and soul. We went to the river bank. The view of the nature was just awesome. Although it was cloudy but the sun blinked from it and spread it's golden rays. Although it was not completely evening but due to clouds it seemed like evening. The grasses of the river bank were dancing by the breeze. The birds were returning to their home. Everything seemed so romantic. I missed Aman. I wished at least I could talk with him right now. But I knew that he was in hospital on his duty. So, I didn't want to bother him.

I thought why I came with them. The climate was too romantic and they should spent time together. But the actual thing was that our elders didn't give them the permission to go for a ride alone together and that's why they took me with them.

We clicked some pictures together. It was a jolly evening. My-brother-in-law addressed me as Punjabi-saali (Punjabi-sister-in-law) as I wore a turban. He was really a nice man. It started raining suddenly and we run towards the car. We got into the car before we got wet. He drove the car slowly towards the home. He drove it slowly as he wanted to reach home late and enjoy the weather with his wife. And for me the weather remined me of Aman. I played a romantic song on my song wearing my earphones in my ear lost in the thought of Aman. I remember all the things from the beginning. Suddenly I remembered the thing that he asked me curiously about what things bother me and why I was upset and depressed. It also impressed me that I never told him about anything then and talked with him with a normal way but still he could sense. I told him everything about my ex and he told me that he also had and he consoled me and encouraged me to start a new life.

Ten

I found my albatross after finding my Aman. I was a phoenix and he gave me a new life a, a beautiful direction to my life. He became my destination and also my journey started with him and I had to complete it with him. Albatross is a bird who lives alone and flies alone until it found it's partner and spends its own life with it's partner. A perfect example of true love and loyalty.

Aman is a pure soul. I felt like he completed me. He set my broken life into a beautiful one. Encouraged me to achieve my goal to fulfil my dream. Once he told me that he would never left my hand until I want his company. And yes, I wanted him for my life time. I love his company and wanted that he could be there for me holding my hands till my last breath. For me he was the blessing of Mahadev. My only wish. I not only got attached with him but also I felt that I was connected. Connected by a infinity bond that binds our relation, that binds our soul, that binds us.

We were like two free souls, just like albatross. We were incomplete without each other. The sky was all ours. No bonds, no boundaries, no limitations, only limitless love. We didn't have to show our love to each other. We could feel that, sense each other's emotions. I remembered the day when he confessed his feelings in front of me. I sensed it before he told but that was unexpected for me the way he confessed it. My mind was full of excitement and surprise. My heartbeat run so fast and even loud that I could hear it. I breathed so deep. When I read his text I could even able to hear his voice. That all were amazing. Just like he pampered me with all his emotions and those feelings showered me with all the love and happiness.

My story was not over here. Every time I remember those memories I relive that moment again. Each time I think of him my face started blushing. When I am writing my story I felt each and every word which holds thousands of emotions.

Eleven

I eagerly waited for the night when the time would come and I would explain to Aman how I felt today and how badly I missed him. Although I wanted to hide my emotions and all feelings from him, but I couldn't. I was dying to tell him all those things.

We returned home but still had no courage to entered into the home as we were too late. We still sat inside the car. "You have boyfriend na? Don't lie." Asked my brother-in-law. "You are too gorgeous, beautiful and smart also. You definitely have."

"She has not. How can be she has a bf? If she has, she didn't cut her hair like boys." My sister replied him.

I took a deep breath and felt a little bit relaxed. They teased me by showing a pic of his brother in relative. But I annoyed them. I was only thinking about Aman.

It was night. We (I, sister and brother-in-law) sat together and chit-chatted. That was a wonderful day and the evening was full of fun. We played ludo and every time brother-in-law did some prank on my sister and cheated her in that game and it became so interesting and too much fun.

Aunt called us for dinner. We all together had our delicious dinner. My sister ate with her mother-in-law on the same plate. It all were hilarious for me. But the thing that amused me more she treated me more lovingly than her own daughter-in-law. After dinner they all left for their home but sister still stayed here some more days as I was there and their in-laws also agreed with it.

My sister came to slept with me and aunt. She (Aunt) hugged me and kissed me on forehead. Told some sort of naughtiness of our childhood and recall those golden memories.

Aman's message beeped on my mobile. I excused them and went to the corner of the bed so that I could talk peacefully.

"Hey sweetheart. How are you?" He said.

"Not really well."

"Why? What happened baby? What's wrong?"

"I missed you so much."

"I miss you too sweetheart."

"You know what happened today. My sister and her husband went for a ride and I was also with them and the weather was also so romantic. I wished you could be here. I miss you so so so much."

"Stupid. Why did you go with them? You should leave them alone na baby." He replied. "Sweetheart you missed me and wished that if my hubby would be here then Ritu also enjoyed the weather and we could also go for a long drive and enjoyed the scenario with hand in hand right?" He teased.

"Yeah." (With a sad emoji) I replied.

"Don't worry baby. I will be coming there to meet you. And at that time you will fulfil all your wishes. Okay!! We will click pictures together, will go for long rides and long walks with hand and hand."

"I wish I can hug you." (With a sad emoji)

"I also have the same wish baby. But what can we do. But whenever I will come you do it okay. We will do everything that you want. I will fulfil all your dreams and wishes. Please don't be upset sweetheart." He consoled me and treaded as if I was a upset child.

We chatted late till midnight or so. We exchanged our numbers. I really missed him too much even I didn't know how badly he was become so important for me that I needed him badly.

Twelve

I returned home. I only chatted with him but neither I talk to him by call nor I seen him in video call. After returning back to my home the relation between us got changed. Means when I left home for aunt's house Aman and I were only best friends but when I returned, the mode of our relation was changed. We were not only boyfriend and girlfriend but also more than that. Mean according to us we were not lovers; we were husband and wife. But after returning to home the frequency of our conversation was very much less than aunt's house. I was unable to come online at night and due to his work load he was unable to talk to me at day. So, we talked very rare; only when he found some time between his duty. I knew all the circumstances but sometimes I really miss him too much that I got angry that he had no time for me. Sometimes I understood everything about the situation but also I couldn't control my anger and texted him harshly. Most of the time he understood my emotions and made me realise the things and made me calm down. But sometimes he also lost his patience and then quarrel took place between us.

"Why don't you understand the things? What's the problem? What are you thinking about me that I am talking with other girls and not with you?" He said disappointedly and harshly.

I knew that his duty was like that, that he had no time for his own. He told me before, about his medical stuffs and also knew that he had no time for having his lunch also. But still I behave like a dumb.

"Maybe I don't know?" I replied harshly.

"What do you mean that may be? You won't trust me."

"I don't mean that."

"Then what do you mean by maybe. You think that I am not giving time to you and flirting with other girls. How can you thought like that. If I have no time for you, not for myself, then how can I give time to other girls."

"I don't mean that. Please listen. I'm sorry dear. I don't want to hurt you. And of course I trust you. You know it na how much I love you and in love trust is the first and most important thing and in long distance trust is everything. Then how could you think that I won't trust you. I trust you baby, even more than myself. I'm really sorry baby. I was disappointed that you have no time for me and I missed you so much. That's why I wrote all those rubbish. I promise I'll never do it again. Please forgive me na." I said him in a very low and guilty tone.

"It's okay sweetheart. But please at least you try to understand my situation. I also miss you and wanna talk to you badly but I'm helpless. I can't do anything. I have no time. I love you." He replied.

"Can u call me now please? I wanna see u badly and no one is in home."

"Okay."

He called me. It was a video call. The very much exciting and special moment for me that it was the first time I was going to see him in real means in a video call. When the call rang on my phone I started breathing heavily and my heart stated beating very fast that I could hear it. I picked up the call but turns off my camera. My hairs were very short so I felt uncomfortable before him as it was our first meet.

He was that much handsome as in his pics. He always wore glasses in his all pics. I saw his eyes for the first time in video call. Such beautiful eyes. Almond shaped deep eyes that one could easily hypnotised by his eyes. I had not seen such beautiful eyes before; I felt. And his smile was the most precious one for me. A bright smile and I just lost myself completely within his smile. I saw him smiling a little bit in his pics but in real it was more beautiful than that. I felt as if something soothing my soul and I felt relief. That type of relief which one can found by finding a cold glass of water in a very hot sunny day.

When I received the call he waved me Hi with a great, beautiful, bright smile. He asked me to open the camera so that he could also see me but I didn't. So, the duration of our call was very short and he cut the call and texted me.

"Why you turned off your camera? How can I see you then?" He told me.

"My hairs are too short. I'm not comfortable with the boy's style haircut." I replied.

"No problem. I love you as you are. Your hairstyle and makeup etc don't matter for me. So, I'll call you now and you have to remain your camera on." He instructed me like as if I was a baby.

He called me again. I received the call with camera on this time. I felt very uncomfortable and shy also. I couldn't even saw him directly into his eyes. When he saw me a satisfactory and bright smile appeared in his face. He saw me continuously for a while then told me by action that my dimples were beautiful. I got overjoyed.

After a long term fight the effect of the video call and the first time experience of seeing each other was much more heart soothing. The most beautiful part of the whole thing was the effort he made to make the misunderstanding clear and to make me happy.

Everything was so special and magical because all were happening for the first time in our lives. The first video call, the first time of hearing each other's voices, our first fight, first misunderstanding, the efforts of both to clear the misunderstanding, the realisation of value and importance of each other and everything.

The more we got closer, the more we knew each other, the more trust built between us and the more I had believed strongly Mahadev. Every time when there was any sort of misunderstanding and we made quarrel I believed that Mahadev set everything correct and perfect and he protect my relation. And I felt it strongly. It was a divine feeling.

Thirteen

When I saw his pic there was a smile automatically appeared on my face and I started blushing. I couldn't control myself not to smile. I collected all his pics and videos. I needn't to ask him for his videos and pics. I collected them from his DP's and whatsapp status and from Instagram stories. I felt something different for him, something special and some heavenly connection type. I felt him even though we didn't even meet. I felt his body smell, his heartbeat in my chest and as if I breath his breathing air. All the things were seemed like imaginary but all things were happening with me.

It was a winter night. I slept next to my mom covering a blanket. All were sleeping in my house but I was still awake and I was trying to sleep. It was too cold outside and the temperature may be 2-3 degree Celsius. I felt the cold inside the room so severely that the thick blanket could not give me appropriate comfort. I was shivering slightly. Suddenly I felt something warm like a warm hug from behind. I turned towards that side and saw that my mom was at the other side of the bed far from me. I still felt that warmth. It felt like as if Aman hugged me tightly. I could smelt his fragrance and feel his breath. At first, I thought that all were only my imaginations but when I kept my mind from Aman then also I smelt that same fragrance. That fragrance was so clear and not the imagination of my mind or neither anyone of our family use that perfume. I thought then as if I was dreaming but I was awake and I felt as if our breath collided and I breathed by his fragrance and the air of his breath gave the life to my breath. I felt his heartbeat in my heart. At first, I felt like there were two hearts beating in my chest at a time. But then it was felt like the heart was mine but the beat was him. I thought as if it was night and maybe I thought such things as in movies, so I felt that. But after that day I could felt those things regularly. Not only in night but also every time. When I placed my hand on my chest I could felt his heartbeat and even I could hear it often and felt it even without placing my hand on chest.

All these things gave me confidence that there could be some Raabta (relation) between us which was beyond our imagination. I felt something bind us and never let us separate. I felt something special and the blessing of Mahadev every time.

Now the frequency of conversation was very much less. Although I was able to come online at night by then but still he talked rarely as he was very much tired by the whole day work. Yes, I missed him, I missed him a lot, dying to talk with him and also got angry when the duration of the days when we didn't talk got longer but I felt him more than that. I understood his problem without even talking and also he understood mine. We understood each other's silence, we felt each other. We sensed each other's mood even without any conversation. It satisfied me most. It made my feelings more stronger.

We talked rare but whenever we talk the conversation lasts for at least 2-3 hours. Those are the most beautiful and romantic hours. We both wanted that my college would reopen soon so that we could talk by phone call comfortably. But the situation of COVID was too pandemic and drastic that there would be no hope for the reopening of college in near future.

I was happy with him, with the moments we spent together. Each time were special for me even though we were unable to talk. Special for me by his thoughts, his memories, his pics, his videos. He mentioned my name in his that social media writing platform where we met. That was a very much special gift for me. I was very happy that day when he wrote my name. We talked that day and I was very happy and also talked with him excitedly. He was very happy as I was happy. He made me feel very special that day. He wrote some more testimonials, shayries and quotes for me. I also wrote and in his testimonial side there were only my testimonials for him. It made me feel more happy. Every time I talked to him and thought about him I loved him more and more and I wanted to tell the whole world that how much I love him. But every time think that might be any evil eye break my relation.

Fourteen

It was an evening. I was sitting at the backyard of my house staring at the sky. I love to stair stars and wonder in their world in my world of imagination. I even love to talk with stars, plants, animals, birds. I love their company and love to share my emotions with them as they don't judge me. I love spending hours beneath the sky at night. I felt as if they were very close to me. Cool relaxing wind blew which somewhere soothed my mind and soul. I felt very relaxed. I enjoyed the moment. Aman's memories made the moment more beautiful. I was lost in his thoughts, the way he talked, the way he tried to hide his feelings from me and still I knew and felt everything. That made my mood more jolly.

The next day I checked his profile in that writing app. I usually checked because I loved to do that as I loved to read his quotes and every time I opened I felt as if I was wonder in his world. And the other reason which made me happy was he wrote my name as life partner in his profile. But that day when I checked it my name was missing in his profile bio. Everything was same as before except my name. It hurt me. I felt as if something pierced my heart so deeply. I thought that he didn't love me anymore or perhaps he might fall in love with someone else. Tears rolled down over my checks. My heart was aching from an unknown pain. As I was in my house and if anyone show me crying then they would ask me the reason and I couldn't explain them. So, I controlled my emotions and pain and wiped up my tears and stopped crying.

I told this to Bini. I explained her everything. Also I told her that perhaps his family came to know about our relation and might be that's why he had to remove my name. I didn't know why I told her this. Might be I felt that. But at that moment the pain of my soul was so deep that I was unable to feel anything or might be the things my heart said to me I couldn't hear or might be didn't want to hear at all. I wanted to ask him and clear all the things but also I didn't want to text him anymore. Bini also suggested me to don't exaggerate the things too much or else they would get more complicated. I considered the things for over millions of times and then finally concluded that I should text him and ask him what's the matter.

We generally talked in Whatsapp but that day I texted him on Instagram as before we talked.

"Hey!! I wanna say sth. If u will fall in love with someone else in any day then plz tell me. Never leave my hand without informing me. I can't leave if u leave me without informimg me. I love u so so so much. And I wanna see u happy always with me or without. So plz ever if it will happen then plz told me." I texted him.

My heart was aching badly. My mind was pondering here and there. I prayed enormously to Mahadev that what I was thinking all to be negative and false. I prayed that the only girl he loved the most to be I. I waited for his reply with a great hope. My heartbeats went very fast each and every time.

"What happened to you? Why will I leave you sweetheart. I love u. only u nd always will be. No one can take ur place in my heart. I love u too darling." He replied.

As soon as his message beeped on my phone screen I checked it like hurricane. His this one message heals every scar and answered all my doubts about his love for me. I neither ask him why he removed my name nor said anything. Just the tears of calmness rolled down on my cheeks. This time the tears were of happiness and enthusiasm.

I remembered the day before some months when I felt the fear of losing him. That was one of the terrible moment of my life. I felt as if I lost him for a moment. After we got into relationship one night he said suddenly that we couldn't be together and he had to go. Our destinations were different. He was a problem himself and he didn't want to drag me into any such of problems. I didn't understood anything. He told all those things all of a sudden and got offline. I texted him a lot and even called him but he didn't answer. I couldn't connect him and started crying. It felt as if I lost him. I didn't get him completely yet but I lost him for the moment. I couldn't understand what to do. I started praying Mahadev and also my tears never stopped rolling down. I continuously crying and praying. After ten minutes he came online and replied my message. He then said me and promised me that he would never gonna leave me alone and never leave my hand until I to him to go from my life by myself.

Fifteen

I was glad that, that was only just a misunderstanding created by myself. The things were nothing like that which type of rubbish I thought. But the question why he removed my name remains in my mind. I didn't want that any type of doubt remain in my mind about him. I wanted to clear everything.

He was some how free one day and we talked for a while. I observed that he was in a good mood. I asked him, "Baby can I ask u sth, if u will never get angry?" He didn't like my questioning nature and he got irritated by it. But he never scold me for it neither forced me to change it.

"Okay. Ask." He replied calmly.

"I didn't tell u to write my name in ur bio. U wrote it by urself. U now removed it also. Don't u know it hurts me."

"Baby listen. I can make u understand everything. My cousin had seen ur name in my Id and told to my mom about it. That's why I have to remove it. I'm really sorry sweetheart. I don't mean to hurt u."

"Did mom scold u? You told me na that ur family have no problem in love or in love marriage. Then what's the problem?"

"I thought that they have no problem with it. But I knew it recently that they don't like it. The main issues are the same like most of the cases like cast, love and we have also some extra like our culture and the distance. All these matters to my family."

"Okay. Then what is your decision?" I asked aggressively with a broken heart.

"Baby I love you. And always will be. They will get agree or not that's not matter. According to me you are my wife and that's all. But I don't know about marriage. But I will try to convince them." He consoled me.

I didn't want to talk to him further. I didn't want to force him for anything. I trusted him more than myself and beyond that I trusted my Mahadev that he never let me down and never let to break my relation and always protected it. I only consoled my heart by saying that he loved me and I felt that and that's enough for me.

Sixteen

I had a strong believe on my feelings that they couldn't betray me. More than that I had a huge faith on Mahadev that he was always there with me and he set everything perfect. Not also my feelings but also I could see the effort Aman made to set everything clear and perfect when we have any sorts of misunderstanding. Though he was too much busy with his work but when any sort of misunderstanding took place he even left his work incomplete to solve it. I had seen this. Then how could I believe that he didn't love me. I often told to my friends about Aman and they told me that he never did love me. He only just made time pass. If he really did he give time to me. Although I didn't tell about Aman to all my friends but those who were very close to me knew about him and those who kept my secrets as secret knew about certain things about us.

Sometimes I also exaggerate the thing when I listened them and then misunderstanding arose. I argued that he had no time for me ruthlessly and for that's why quarrel took place. When I kept all the things between me and Aman secret then my life and relation went on smoothly but when I revel something then problem got arose. I didn't say that they were my enemies and they couldn't see me happy. But the things were that every person has different point of view and as they were my friends and also my well-wishers they always wanted to see me in pain. But the things were also like that which I felt and I could see they didn't. So, neither they were wrong nor I.

Seventeen

It was the month of December. We talked hardly but whenever we talked it become the beautiful memory for me to live other days with it, smoothly. He was quite free on 29 and we talked very long. I wished him to be with him on New Year's Eve and wanted to be available for me that day. I was very happy and waiting for New Year's Eve.

New Year's Eve: 10 pm sharp I texted him "Hey! How long it takes you to be free?"

No reply …

15 minutes later …

"Are you there??"

Again, no reply …

Half an hour later …

"Are you coming or not?"

"Wait for a while. M working." Aman replied.

"So, u r not coming?"

"No, I'll be there. Just wait. Let me finish my work."

I waited for him more than one hour. Each second during that time felt like ages. Don't know why it bothered me a lot. With passing time my anger started increasing. And finally, he texted, "Yo."

"So, r u free now?"

"Yeah."

"What take you so long to free on New Year's Eve?"

"Nothing. Some home works and that's it."

I felt his breath heavy although we weren't by each other's side and we had a distance of miles. He even didn't talk much. We planned a lot of things to do that night but we did nothing. He didn't tell me what happened to him. I sensed that he was bothered by something and I want to know the reason but he didn't share anything with me. I convinced him but I failed. After too much effort at last I lost my patience and then I treated him harshly. I didn't know what happened to me at that time and why I behaved like despo although I knew Aman's state of mind was not good. At 11:55 pm, only just before 5 minutes of the New Year I said him harshly "I don't wanna talk to you. BYE!!!"

He didn't say a word. I waited for him that might be he would reply. I thought at least he wished me Happy New Year first. But he didn't. At 12:00 am sharp he put a status of HAPPY NEW YEAR!!! and then got offline. I waited and waited and waited but he didn't wish me. My friends and relatives started wishing but he didn't and it hurt me a lot.

Yes, it hurts when you except something special from your special one but you didn't get it.

Lastly, I wished him. As it was my first New Year with him so, I wanted everything to be special and memorable. I wished to wish him first and I did it. Although our first New Year was not good. I called Bini in the morning to wish and Guddu was also on with conference. I told her to took a conference with Aman as I didn't call him directly and also I wanted to wish him directly through phone call. She diel the number and he answered it also after some ring. But when he knew that it was me he behaved harshly and cut the call. By his behaviour I got hurt a lot and my eyes got teary and voice got chocked. I didn't continue the conversation with Bini and Guddu and cut the call. I wanted to hide my tears but it was very much difficult task for me for the moment.

I consoled myself. Then I called him a video call. He answered and asked what happened. My eyes filled with water and seeing this he got angry and asked what happened and why I was crying. I said nothing but just looked at him. His face was faded and he was doing his duty and busy with his work but his face gave coolness to my eyes. He cut the call. At that moment I realised that I was so stupid last night that I created another dumb scene before him. I already knew that he was bothered by something but still I behaved like a despo and irritated him.

And he was such a gentle man that despite his personal problem he came online last night only for me and what I did?? I want to apologize but he didn't even want to talk to me now.

Eighteen

It's been 15 days from the New Year and we didn't talk. Aman didn't talk with me and neither told me about his problem. He was so busy with his problems that he had no time for another stuff. I knew it but still I want to know the root of the problem and I couldn't see him upset or bothered. I wanted to contact him so many times but he replied the same thing every time, "Leave me alone. I need space. I have to solve my problems by myself and when everything will be fine I will definitely text you." And it was my problem that I had not that much patience to wait and in this stupidity of mine I created more problems for him.

I thought he was not comfortable with me to share that problem; probably he would share this with Misthy. I called her.

"Hey!! R u free?" With a sobbing sound.

"Why r u crying? What happened?" Misthy asked surprisingly.

"Plz help me Misthy …Plz…" Crying aloud.

"Stop crying and tell me what happened?" She told me.

"Aman is not talking with me since 1st Jan. I don't know what happened but I'm sure he has some personal problem but he is not telling what happened."

"So, what's the issue? Why r u crying. Give him some space na. Everything will be fine and he will talk to you also very soon."

"No, I can't. I don't have that much patience. Plz do sth. I want u to talk to him."

"Why? No plzz!!" She asked surprisingly.

"Plz don't deny. Plz Yaar…. plz…"

"Okay I'll. But first of all, stop crying." She replied.

Nineteen

"Ritu! You don't need to love him. Just leave that man okay. He is such a shit man. If he will be the last option then also you don't have to love him. Stay single but don't love him." Misthy said angrily.

"What happened? Why are you talking like this?" I asked her curiously.

"You know what Ritu, he doesn't deserve you. And you deserve much more better. According to me he is just waste of time and that's it. So many boys love you and also they keep you happier if you choose one of them. Aman even doesn't love you."

"What the hell Misthy. What the hell you are saying. Mind your language. And tell me briefly what happened? Did you call him or what?"

My anger was at peak. I couldn't listen anything against Aman and she told a lot.

"Yeah I called him and you know what he was so rude and he was not interested to listen any kind of your stuff. And when I told him that you stop eating he said it was your problem and your father's problem. Ritu leave him. He doesn't deserve you okay!!!"

I just cut the call and tears rolled down from my eyes. I was speechless and my mind was completely blank.

I decided to leave him. But is it easy to move on after knowing the actual reason? Yes, of course it was my fault not his. I should not bother him and I should understand his situation. If I saw the whole situation with someone else's eyes then it was seen that Aman didn't love me but as I knew him more than anyone else and even I could feel his love then how could I believe that he didn't love me. I thought then, was it my true love? Did I love him truly when I didn't want to understand his situation? No, I shouldn't leave him. I should give him time and also I had to give some time to our relationship... Let I be quite for sometime and take time to the time to be everything okay. And I should keep my relation private and shouldn't involve anyone.

I just prayed Mahadev to set everything fine. I didn't want to lose Aman nor did I can see him in pain. He was that precious jewel for me, my happy place which I always wish for. It hurt me when I felt his pain. He never told me what bothers him or he was in pain. But how can it be hide from me. I sensed he had any sorts of problem but I felt everything. And that's why I always felt that there was a very strong connection between us. He didn't tell me anything cause he didn't want to make me tense.

After a long while I finally texted him, "How are you? Is everything fine now?"

"I'm fine. I'll talk to you soon. Don't worry." He replied.

I felt he was somehow okay than before. I felt relaxing and decided not to bother him and texted, "Take care."

It was a great relief when you sensed that your loved person is okay and everything is in a progressive manner and the situation is under control.

I usually used to text him good morning after I woke up and good night before went to sleep there after. And he also replied me. We didn't talk anything expect that, not a single word.

One night I texted him, "Good ni8. Take care." As I did daily. He was in a good mood that day. He started the conversation as good night but further proceed that and it continued very long. I was very happy that everything was fine now. I thanked Mahadev for that. That day I believed that I should not involve anyone in my love life and I should believe in by own feelings cause they never betray me and put faith on Mahadev; he heals everything.

Twenty

It was 1st Feb evening. I was wondering outside my house enjoying the spring. Spring made the earth jolly. Wind was refreshing with a chill twist and the chirping sound of birds were so relaxing. Everything made one's mood calm, peaceful and refreshing.

I returned home after 6 pm when evening said goodbye and night said hello to the earth. I got fresh and checked my phone. What I saw was just surprizing. I couldn't believe my eyes. How could it be possible! It was Aman's call which made me so surprized. Three miscall from Aman's number. He never called me before; even he didn't text me first then how did it happened. At that time my father returned home from market and suddenly asked my brother about me. Hearing that he was asking about me I start shivering in fear. I thought might he got to know about or what happened. I went online immediately to ask Aman that what happened and why he called me. He texted me, "Hi" by his own and there also a miscall. I asked him, "Aman, What happened? Why did you call me so many times?"

Seen but no reply.

"Aman what happened told me. Is everything fine?"

Again, seen but no reply.

My fear increased.

"Why don't u reply?"

I got a call from him then but I cut it.

"Papa is at home. Don't call me now."

He now called me in whatsapp.

I received the call.

"Hello."

No answer from the other side.

Again- "Hello!"

Again, silence from his side.

I cut the call and texted, "What the hell is going on can u plz tell me?"

This time also seen but no reply.

I called him in whatsapp.

"Hello." I heard a tone of a stranger but not Aman.

"Hello? Who's this?"

"Bhabi Namaste. I'm Aman's friend." He said.

"Namaste. But, where is he? Is everything alright? Is he fine? Why you received his call?" I asked with a fear in my heart.

"Yeah Bhabi he is alright. He just put his phone on charging and went outside and you called him, and that's why I received the call." He replied.

"Okay!!!" I said and cut the call.

After sometime I texted him, "When Aman will return then plz told him to text me."

Seen immediately.

A call from his number on my whatsapp.

"What's your problem? Where are you texting too much? Don't you know it's my working time?" He said angrily.

"Why did you call me then?"

"When did I call you. Did you lost it?"

I sent him the screenshots of my call list and asked him pointing his number, "Is this not your number?"

"Yeah this is mine but I didn't call you. And don't behave like a stupid further."

"If you have always a problem with me then why don't you block my number?" I told him angrily.

"That will be fine." He replied angrily.

He told something to me but I didn't even listen and cut the call.

He blocked me in whatsapp.

Twenty-one

This time my anger was at peak. I didn't call him nor texted him to unblock me. But I waited for him to unblock me. It's one day completed but he didn't unblock me. I waited and waited and waited. Two days completed but still he didn't unblock me. Now my anger turned into love for him as two days passed for our fight and my anger was also vanished. And as he blocked me it hurt me and my love for him got outside from me in the form of tears.

I texted him on Instagram, "Don't you able to unblock me?"

After few hours he replied, "It's your decision that I should block you."

"Now I want that you will unblock me." I argued.

"Okay, fine! Don't shout!"

He unblocked me and I took a breath of relief.

"Your friend told me Bhabi that day." I told him with excitement.

Being Bhabi for the friend of your loved one was another level of happiness and excitement. He thought I didn't like that his friend called me Bhabi and I complained before him about that "Don't mind his words." He told me.

But I was very much happy when his friend called me that. Equal level of happiness when he called me sweetheart and his friend called me Bhabi.

Twenty-two

With passing time I realised that we needn't to know all the answers of all the questions and all the reasons of all the actions. Love is like devotion. The more we prayed from pure heart the more we being blessed and the more we get the pure form of love. Aman didn't tell me everything. He just avoided the things. But in other way he taught me the actual meaning of life and how to live it and deal with the difficult phases of life. Indirectly he taught me all tough lessons of life. More appropriately he took tests of life from me like Mahadev took tests from Parvati. I realized the things later.

I eagerly waited for the day when my college would reopen and finally the day came. Government declared to reopen schools and colleges. It was 10th of Feb when my college reopens. But, no one went to hostel on the day of reopening according to the nature of human hosteller. I and my best friend Guddy – only we two went to the hostel on the day of hostel reopening.

All hostel was empty and the warden was also not there. We found it more fun to spent the night at hostel without any guardian cause we could do whatever we want. And my hostel rules were very strict and if there were any warden then she could tell us and guide us. But now we were our own's guide. Although we didn't go outside the hostel only sat on the balcony of my room and enjoyed the night view from there with a slow music. The cold breeze blew, music was on in my phone and the climate was peaceful. The perfect climate that I always craving for. I diel Aman's number. I didn't know why but he didn't talk to me nicely and it hurt me. I cut the call and tears started rolled down from my eyes. His that sots for behaviour hurt me a lot.

After some time Aman called me. I picked up the phone.

"Hey!!"

"What?" I asked angrily.

"Do I bother you?" He asked teasingly.

"Don't you know it?" I asked angrily.

"Tell me. I bother you?"

"Of course you do."

"So, you don't love me?"

"I don't know." I answered.

"Tell me!! Don't you love me?" He teased me again.

"I think you know it better." I answered.

"I love you."

I didn't say anything.

"Sweetheart I love you." He said again sweetly.

"Why do you always made me cry? Why do you always hurt me?" I asked him with sobbing.

"Sweetheart I love you so so so much." He said even more sweetly now.

"I'm not going to tell you I love you."

"Sweetheart! I love you."

The sweetness in his voice melts my heart and vanished my anger.

"I also love you."

And our conversation continues.

Our mode of conversation was so sweet and then turned romantic. We talked for a very long time till 2am. It was Propose day of Valentines week. He wished me, "Happy propose day." That was the best night ever.

"I want to marry you." He said. "Will you marry me?"

"Are you sure Aman?" I asked excitedly.

"Yes, my sweetheart." He replied. "Will you be my wife?"

I loved it when he called me "MINE".

"Yes." I replied.

I was so happy that my happiness has no boundaries.

That moment was so romantic. His tone was so sweet. The moon was on the sky witnessing our love, shone brighter and seemed like it was bigger than usual. He video called me by himself without even I was asking for. Number of times I cut the call and he called me back. He wanted to see me, my face, my action. He did my mimicry, kissed me, teased me in the name of ghost. That night was so romantic and the best night ever.

Twenty-three

I was very much happy. That night as if he showered his all love on me.

It was a very bright morning. Guddy and I woke up at 9am. We got fresh and went to the market for breakfast. When we returned to hostel, I told her about last night. She was very happy as she knew it well that I usually didn't talk with him. Other girls of the hostel had come by the afternoon. The hostel was full, crowded and noisy after one year again because college classes were suspended due to COVID for one year.

I waited for the night when I would got chance to call Aman again. And finally, night arrived and it's 10 pm when it was the time to call him. But when I called him he didn't talk with me. After that day this continues regularly. I waited for him whole day that when the night came and when I would talk with him; but every time he received the call talked with me harshly then cut the call. Those nights were turned painful and sleepless for me. I was unable to understand the sudden changes in him. He didn't want to talk to me either. Every night brought only tears for me.

The days were painful also. He wasn't with me. His stranger behaviour was killing me. Every night I called him, he answered the call also; but we didn't talk to each other. If we talked then we fought only. The days were very tough for me as I was being alive only with his memories but not with him. I wanted to tell him that how much I got hurt by his behaviour. I often cry before him but even my crying, my tears were valueless for him. I loved to being quite instead of telling how much it hurt. I started writing my pains in a diary and name that before him. When I wrote in it I felt as if I told my pains to Aman. When I got hurt by him everyday I went to the balcony and cry and prayed Mahadev to set everything well. I started fasting on every Monday without even any liquid food wishing that my relation would be fine soon. I never cried before anyone although I hurt a lot cause if I did then they would tell against of Aman and that was more painful than anything else.

My Aman was not wrong neither he hurt me. But the thing was that I expect something from him which was not fulfilled by him and that's why I got hurt and absolutely that was not his fault. He was such a sweet man.

Twenty-four

It was an auspicious day Mahashivratri. I believed Mahadev so much that the day was very special for me. I waited very excited for this day. I never did fasting before on Mahashivratri. On Mahashivratri it was a two days fasting programme. The day before Mahashivratri I did fasting but drank water. I was so much excited that I never slept the whole night in waiting for the morning for go to temple. I am usually a night owl and don't wakeup early in the morning in my life. But that day I woke up at 4 am. First I cleaned my room in hostel then got fresh and took a shower. Then I got woke up Guddy. She then went to the bathroom. When she returned from bathroom after bath she saw me sitting on the bed completely lost in music and smiling like an idiot. She called me five times and then I listen to her.

"You know what, I thought to ask you for pressing my clothes but after seeing you in this condition I don't wish to disturb and disrupt from your important work." She teased me.

"What important work?" I asked surprisingly as I did nothing.

"Cause, I can see you that you are lost in Aman's thought through music and I don't want to disturb you." She laughed naughtily.

As I read in a private college so there was no holidays and we had to go to college daily except Sundays. We got ready and went to college by college bus. When I was on the way I texted Aman to send any of his pic. I arrived at college and rushed toward the classroom to check my phone as if he sent his pic or not. For my luck he sent. When I saw it felt like as if I saw directly my Mahadev. I was very happy as on an auspicious day I had the chance to saw my Mahadev, my husband, my Aman.

From the day we got into a relationship I considered Aman as my hubby and he also considered me and treated me as his wife. And our relation was like husband-wife relation not a girlfriend-boyfriend relation. And in my heart there was only one person although I had a lot of male friends but all my love was only for him. When I got hurt by him then also sometimes I became happy because in my heart there was only place for Aman weather it was love or pain. Only he had that right no one else except him.

From college one mam took all the girls to Trinath temple. I wished very much to go to the temple and Mahadev fulfilled my that wish. Even it was more appropriate that on that day Mahadev fulfilled my all wishes. I prayed Mahadev for Aman and for our relationship that continues for eternity. I wished in my mind that might be in the occasion of Mahashivratri I wanted to talk with my hubby without any fight peacefully and see him on videocall. Usually whenever I asked Aman for videocall he denied. So, I texted him with a fear.

"Can you call me a videocall after some time? I wanna see you."

"Okay." He replied.

After sometime he called but I couldn't receive the call as I was still in college and it was time for went to hostel. I texted him to said some more time.

"I'll call you after arriving at hostel within 10 min." I texted.

I feared that he would deny as he did it usually.

"Okay." He replied.

I couldn't believe to my eyes when I saw it. It was unbelievable for me. I run towards my room when reached the hostel. I just threw my bag to my bed and then called him. He received. He was in hospital in his duty.

"Hi! Whatsup." He said with a smiling face.

"Hii!!" I replied.

My happiness had no boundaries.

I talked him for a while then cut the call. I wished him to talk at night and he agreed also. I broke my fast after 10:30 pm after eating prasad of Mahadev. I called Aman.

"Hey! When will you get free." I asked.

"I'm in the temple. I can't call you tonight. But I will text you okay." He replied normally and then cut the call.

I waited for him. He came online at 11:30 pm.

"Are u awake and waiting for me?" He asked.

"Yes, of course."

"But I'm so tired baby. Can we talk tomorrow."

"Are you gonna talk with me tomorrow also?"

"Yes."

"Okay then. Goof ni8. Take care."

"Good night sweetheart !!!" He replied.

Twenty-five

Again, the same thing happened. He started avoiding me, his behaviour got harsh for me. He was like a surprize packet. His behaviour and mood swings were mystery for me. I told one of my hostel friend Rinki to talk with him so that perhaps I could know his problem. He talked with her nicely and started teasing me by her name. I let Rinki talked with him from my phone. He told her about his ex and when Rinki told me about that it hurt me a lot. By Rinki's words I felt that as if he had feelings for his ex now also. I wanted Aman's happiness most. It didn't matter with whom he would get happy. Although it hurt me if he like someone else but it's okay in front of his happiness.

My mood was not good and I sat on the balcony after returning from college. Some honeybees suddenly flew towards me. Seeing this I run towards my room but before I could enter into my room and shut the door one honeybee bite on my shoulder. My shoulder swallowed immediately and then it started hurting so much. My hostel friends informed to college and my uncle took me to the hospital. After returning from hospital I texted Aman about that.

At night I told Rinki to call him and informed him about the incident. When Rinki called him first of all asked about my condition.

"How did it happen with her? Is she a small baby that these types of incidents happened with her? She was dancing with the bees or what?" He asked Rinki angrily.

He asked Rinki to give me the phone.

"Take rest and don't cry. Everything will be fine. Take medicines and do first aid and don't use mobile and go to sleep now." He instructed me.

That night I felt that how much he loved me and care for me. He didn't show me that he cared for me but that day his worry about me proved everything.

When I went to bed I remembered the things that proved that Aman actually loved me. One day he teased me by the name of Rinki that she was so sweet and he asked me her number. I cut the call angrily and blocked him on whatsapp. He called me back and talked so sweetly and made me believe that he only loved me.

There was also some reason for his toughness and wired behaviour. He was only 22 and he has the responsibilities of his family, he had to work hard for more than 12 hours. He had no holidays even on festivals. He was studying his masters also. So, it was obvious that his behaviour was rude. But who knew him very well could know how beautiful and soft his heart was.

Twenty-six

Although small small things and my strong feelings for him made me realised and built confidence in me that Aman truly loved me but his harsh behaviour hurt me a lot and created doubt on my mind about his love. After one big fight he blocked me on Instagram and that online writing app where our love story started. His behaviours always hurt me. And these types of work created doubt. He knew it very well that I would never gonna leave him and that's why now he didn't even convinced me when I got angry. I got angry by myself and I got convinced by myself also. It sounds so stupid but it's true.

Once I saw him mentioning his two friends on a status and I got his friends Instagram Id there. I texted his friend Mahakaal only to know about Aman that what was his problem. I introduced myself to Mahakaal as Aman's girlfriend and told him that I wanted to know about Aman that what bothers him. I addressed Mahakaal as brother. First of all he told about Aman that his family was very rude and his family problem and work pressure was the only issue of this kind of behaviour of Aman. Then he wanted to get closer to me. He told me against of Aman that he was a cheater, a flirter and was not a good guy and didn't love me. He told me all these things promising in the name of Mahadev. He told me that he was also a devotee of Mahadev so he couldn't lie using the name of Mahadev. I got to know about his bad intensions from his talks that he wanted Aman and my breakup. He also told me, "You needn't have to cry for Aman. You should did breakup with him. He is a bad guy and don't love you I swear. Leave him and I'll be there for you. Even if you want me as your boyfriend then I'll be, only for you. If you want me to kiss you, I'll do that. I care for you, love you, support you more than Aman."

Listening all these things I feel very low. I also feel bad for Aman. To whom Aman considered as a very good friend, as own brother he cheated him on his backside. He was that snake that bite him with his sense. I stopped talking with Mahakaal. I wanted to tell all these things to Aman but then I thought perhaps Aman might not believe and due to this our relation got worse. I chose to stay silent instead of telling him anything. But I couldn't see him being got involved into problem so I informed him a little bit that he shouldn't believe everyone around him even to his friends also.

When Aman got to know that I talked with his friend he told me angrily, "Didn't you know me? Didn't I tell you about myself? Then why will you involve him in our matter?"

That day I felt how much he actually loved me. That day I realised that no one was happy to seeing us happy or together. Everyone tried to separate us; both his friends as well as mine. The only thing that created misunderstanding and problem in our relation is that the comparison of my love with others and listening to others and involving any third person, listening another's advice. I shouldn't do that. Everyone is unique and every love story is special. I decided not to tell anyone except Mahadev about Aman and about my problems. I started believing my feelings and the magic of Mahadev more than anything else. As always Mahadev protected my relation and will protect it in future also.

Twenty-seven

COVID cases were again started increasing. Our college again got suspended. My mom went to college to bring me back home. And finally, I was at home after two months.

I didn't text Aman as I was angry at him. His behaviour and his friends opinion about him – all these things hurt me a lot and made me upset. I want that Aman would clear the misunderstanding but at the same time I didn't want to talk with him. After 15 days when my anger got cool down I finally texted him. I was in pain and all the things hurt me so much.

"Your friend told me that you don't love me and you have other girlfriends. Is it true?" I asked.

"No. It's not true. You still don't know me. I have only one girl in my life and that's you. Yeah I have girls in my friend circle but I don't love any of them." He replied.

"Don't ever cheat me okay. I love you." I said him sadly.

"I love you too sweetheart." He replied.

"Don't go so far from me plz. It's hurting me and also always created misunderstanding."

"Baby! I think we shouldn't get too close and start to maintain distance from each other." He told.

"Why? What happened?"

"My family fixed my marriage."

"What? u r kidding ri8?"

"No. I'm serious." He replied.

"When is your marriage? Who's the girl?" I asked sadly.

"I don't know."

"U r lying."

"No, I'm not."

"Don't you tell your family about us?"

"They don't listen anything then why will I told them."

"Fine then." I told angrily.

"We shouldn't talk after my marriage."

"Of course."

His words pierced deep into my heart. My mind was blank. I couldn't think anything. Whole night I cried. I prayed Mahadev for giving my Aman back to me and to protect my relation and to don't break it. I didn't sleep the whole night. I finally texted him at 3:12 am, "Please don't go Aman. Please don't leave me. I can't leave without you. Tell your family about us." I begged him and I never begged anyone before. My pain increased each second. It felt like someone pressed a pillow against my face and I couldn't breath. Life hurt me more than death.

88

Twenty-eight

"I can't do anything. Don't go mad." He replied in the morning.

I prayed Mahadev the whole night and in the morning also. I convinced Aman. I didn't understand how could it be happened. I had no believe in his words. But finally he told we would be together till the situation arose when we had to marry another guy. I was quit happy with that also.

When I was in college then also once Aman told me that our love remains forever but marriage was not possible. And due to this we fought many times before. But now I had a faith on Mahadev that he never separates us and our story wouldn't left incomplete.

After that day everything was fine between us. He talked with me regularly on every Saturday. Everything was fine between us. I kept my relation completely private. We both were happy with each other. I stopped arguing, stop asking unnecessary questions, and often stopped doing those works which bothered him. I wanted to be a supportive wife as he considered me as his wife. I wanted to be a better-half in genuine words. He taught me to live present moment, to enjoy each moment instead of being bothered for the future.

Twenty-nine

"Ritu. Give me a pillow. Fast!!" My uncle shouted from outside. I gave him a pillow. "What happened Chachu!!" I asked curiously. "Nona got hospitalized. He can't breath and his condition is very critical." He told and left. My father and uncle brought my grandpa to the hospital and after some medical tests he was identified as COVID positive. His lungs got damaged 92% and his chance of recovery was only 1%. When I heard the news it was hard for me to face the situation as grandpa was very much close to me. I loved him the most. I informed it to Aman. Although he was very much busy with his work but still he consoled me and increased my courage that everything would be fine soon. Grandpa was hospitalized for a week and that was the toughest time for me. I was unable to console myself and getting weaker. I need Aman very much to hold me and my strength and being there for me. And for the whole week till his death Aman was with me and did all the things which I want although I didn't expect. He did everything perfectly even more than I thought. When grandpa left us then that was the most painful moment for me and that was a mental shock which was very difficult for me to bear or face. But then also Aman was there with me like holding me into his arms and consoling me.

Thirty

Aman was too busy with his work that he didn't get time to talk with me. I waited for him and after 17 days I texted him, "When will you come?"

"I don't know. But very soon." He replied.

After that we didn't talk for over a month. Neither I texted nor he. He put some sad status which bothered me. Those status seemed like he loved someone else and he put those for another girl but not for me. I got hurt by thinking all these things. it made me upset, disturbed and angry. I texted him and only due the this we again fought.

This was such a rubbish that we fought over such silly reasons and things that I though. The things might not happened and I was also not sure but we fought only cause I imagined. I realized the thing that even one small misunderstanding can destroy a beautiful relationship within a minute. For all our fights misunderstandings and everything those were painful, only I was responsible for those not he. Love is not like the things to show or to prove or to compare. It is such a beautiful feeling only to feel. That's Aman who made me realise what love actually is.

It was 18th of July Aman's birthday. I waited eagerly for this day. I started preparation before one month although we were very much far from each other and I planned to wish him first. I waited for 12:00 am to wish him although I was very sleepy. During the time when I waited, each moment became special and turned magical for me. I wished him at 12:00 am sharp and he was also very happy with that. That moment was blissful. I could feel his happiness when we talked only for few minutes. When I felt that he was happy it felt like my all wishes got fulfilled. I was very happy. I was very much excited for his birthday even more than that of mine.

After some days it was my birthday and I wanted that he wished me first but he didn't. He even forgot mine and it made me upset. At 6 pm he wished me. He was the last one to wish me but it's okay. I waited for him to wish me and when he wished my happiness had no boundaries. I got very excited and forgot all my anger. We even talked for a while that day after a long time.

I learned so many things from Aman. In actual means he taught me the actual meaning of love and life. We needn't have to talk with each other daily only to remember that he/she is my person and we love each other. Even we should talk when we really want to and need each other the most. If we love each other it doesn't mean that we have to interfere in each other's life, each other's personal stuffs. If we love someone then we should understand him/her and set them free to live his/her life. True love means only we want the happiness of our loved one's no matter what the cost is!!!

And finally, we are going to complete one year. Our happy one year. Yes, although so many obstacles and problem arose in our journey and we had to bear so much pain but that was also precious gift for me as it was the gift from my loved one. I could only wish that the day will never come into our lives when we have to separate from each other and our love continues till eternity. He is my ALBATROSS and always will be!!!

www.ingramcontent.com/pod-product-compliance
Lightning Source LLC
LaVergne TN
LVHW050417160726
843469LV00041B/1119